The Treasure of Amelia Island

The Treasure of
Amelia Island

M.C. Finotti

Pineapple Press, Inc.
Sarasota, Florida

For my mother, Dorothy E. Carbone

Inquiries should be addressed to:

Pineapple Press, Inc.
P.O. Box 3889
Sarasota, Florida 34230

www.pineapplepress.com

Finotti, M.C.
    The treasure of Amelia Island / M.C. Finotti. -- 1st ed.
    p. cm.
    Summary: On Amelia Island in Spanish-ruled Florida in 1813, a treasure hunt causes trouble for ten-year-old Mary and her racially mixed family, whose freedom is being threatened by Pariots from nearby Georgia despite the best efforts of Mary's mother, an African princess called Ana Jai Kingsley.
    ISBN 978-1-56164-416-2 (hardcover : alk. paper)
    1. Florida--History--Spanish colony, 1784–1821--Juvenile fiction. [1. Florida--History--Spanish colony, 1784–1821--Fiction. 2. Family life--Florida--Fiction. 3. Freedmen--Fiction. 4. Slavery--Fiction. 5. Racially mixed people--Fiction. 6. Buried treasure--Fiction. 7. Kingsley, Anna, 1793-1870--Fiction. 8. Amelia Island (Fla.)--History--19th century--Fiction.] I. Title.
    PZ7.F49845Tre 2008
    [Fic]—dc22

                                                                                              2007042686

Hb ISBN-13: 978-1-56164-416-2
Pb ISBN-13: 978-1-56164-536-7

First Edition
Hb 10 9 8 7 6 5 4 3 2
Pb 10 9 8 7 6 5 4 3 2 1

Printed in the United States of America

Prologue

The Christmas I turned eleven an alligator nearly ate my older brother George. For years afterward, the memory of that gator attack colored my birthday like blood oranges in ambrosia. That's the special dessert we used to eat every Christmas when my mother, Ana Jai, picked the oranges with the bright red insides from her favorite tree.

Before the gator attacked George, my mouth would water as I waited for Ana Jai to dish me up a serving of ambrosia. I'd spoon a juicy bite of fruit, sugar, and grated coconut into my mouth and the orange would explode with a tart taste all its own, red juice squirting from my lips. Then my teeth would find the coconut, nutty but sweet, adding another level of delight.

A few days after the gator attacked George, I tried to eat Ana Jai's holiday dessert. It landed in my stomach like a turnip. The ambrosia tasted same as always, but its bright, red color reminded me of the blood pouring from George's ankle.

George wasn't with us for that Christmas dinner. Neither

was Father or our younger half-brother, Diego. It was only my older sister Martha and me—I'm Mary—and Ana Jai forcing us to eat. Martha and I felt like criminals heading for our execution.

It's funny how food can take you back in an instant to another time, another place. In this case, ambrosia takes me back to December 1813, the time we fled from Ana Jai's plantation in La Florida and headed for Amelia Island. That's where we tried to find a treasure and almost lost George.

Our lives changed quickly in that single month, and in the years to follow we talked a lot about how that could happen. George believed it all started with the arrival of Gullah Jack. Truth be told, George never liked Jack all that much, and it figures he'd look to blame him. Jack, you see, is the one who told us of the pirate's treasure buried on Amelia Island and there's no doubt George and I and Diego were drawn to that treasure like mosquitoes to soft skin.

Still, I think our lives began to unravel when we fled Mandarin in the middle of the night. We ran from Patriots, real and imagined, because we were Loyalists to the Spanish crown. And Patriots from up Georgia way wanted to kick us out of La Florida forever, even if it meant they had to kill us.

I used to wonder why Ana Jai couldn't just be a Patriot. We would have been a whole lot safer. But the older I got the more I understood why she could never be anyone but who she was.

In the end, Amelia Island finally gave us a treasure. It just wasn't what we expected to find. This treasure, though, proved far more valuable than anything we ever dreamed of digging up.

1

Ana Jai was like a storm back then, determined to control her destiny with a fury that could change the landscape. Maybe that's why we never called her "mother." Ana Madgigine Jai Kingsley is more or less the name her father, a king in Senegal, gave her when she was born. Minus the Kingsley, of course. That she got from my father, Zephaniah.

Ana Jai was a tall, black-skinned beauty when my parents met, a West African princess who was captured when warring tribesmen raided her father's village. She was only thirteen and to this day she still wears the thirteen silver bracelets her father gave her on her thirteenth birthday. It was a sign of his royalty, his wealth, and his love. It was also the last birthday present she ever received from him.

After she was captured, her enemies sold her to European slave traders for guns and rum. The traders eventually put her in the hold of a ship and sent her to Cuba. Ana Jai said it's a wonder she didn't die of starvation.

"That journey filled me with hate. That's how I survived. I ate hate."

In Cuba, Ana Jai went on the auction block and my father Zephaniah, a ship captain and slave trader, bought her. He took her on another long voyage to Laurel Grove, his first plantation in La Florida.

"Mary, to love a king is not bad," Ana Jai once told me. "But a king who loves you is better."

"Did you make that up?" I asked.

"No, it's an African proverb. My mother told it to me."

It's a great sadness for Ana Jai that she doesn't know what happened to her mother or her father or the rest of her tribe when she was captured. So she calls George and Martha and me her tribe of mulattoes. We have light brown skin, not as dark as her own, but not nearly as white as our father's.

"Your skin's as sweet as orange blossom honey," she used to say to me.

And not to brag or anything, but we are indeed pleasing to the eye. George, sixteen, is tall like Ana Jai, much taller than Father. Martha, fifteen, is prettiest, with Father's bright blue eyes. And me, eleven, I have a head of ringlets that turn partly yellow in the sun. None of us, thankfully, have skin like Father's that turns bright red and peels away when he forgets to wear his sun hat.

When she got to Laurel Grove, Ana Jai quickly learned English and Spanish, the two languages spoken in La Florida, and she learned to read. A Catholic priest from St. Augustine baptized her and taught her reading because he wanted her to read the Bible.

After seven years as a slave, my father freed her, as was Spanish custom. And he freed me and Martha and George then too. I was just a baby so I don't remember much, but I know the day my mother got her freedom is the day she became a Loyalist. She was a big believer in the Spanish way of setting your slaves free after they had worked hard for you for a time.

Ana Jai became my father's partner, helping him train Africans to wash and cook, spin Sea Island cotton, and run a household. They sold these well-trained Africans to rich people in New York City and Boston for a whole lot of money. My mother also owned slaves of her own who lived with us at Mandarin. Two worked inside the house, cooking and such. The rest worked the fields picking Sea Island cotton and oranges and making sugar from sugar cane.

I once asked Ana Jai how she could keep slaves when she was once a slave herself. A frown creased her brow.

"The work would never get done around here without them," she said. "My father had slaves in Africa. I will free mine one day, just like him."

She also knew firsthand that freedom wasn't easy for freed persons. They often found themselves poor and in danger. Still, I think it bothered her, keeping slaves, even if she wouldn't admit it.

At least Ana Jai actually freed her slaves one day, unlike that former president of the United States, Thomas Jefferson. Ana Jai said he discoursed about the evils of slavery, yet still owned 187 slaves. In anger, she took the "T" out of her original name, Anta. She didn't want to have anything in common with Thomas Jefferson, not even the letter "T."

"Are you getting rid of the 'J' you share with him too?" I asked.

"No, I must keep that. It's all I have of my father."

And because she planned to free her slaves, Ana Jai would not allow us to use the word slave. She did not like the word Negro either.

"These are Africans," Ana Jai insisted. "When they earn

their freedom they can return to Africa."

So, we did as we were told. We called them Africans, even though some of them had never stepped foot in Africa and probably never would.

2

We hardly knew Father back then. He lived on the west side of the St. Johns River at Laurel Grove Plantation with hundreds of Africans. We lived on the opposite side of that wide, wide river at Mandarin, a much smaller plantation with far fewer Africans. It was as far from Father as Ana Jai could get and still maintain business dealings with him.

Ana Jai named her plantation Mandarin because of the twenty Mandarin orange trees and one blood orange tree she planted there. The governor of La Florida, Juan de Estrada, gave Ana Jai the orange seeds and the land after Father gave us our freedom papers. The governor said it was Ana Jai's reward for being loyal to the king of Spain.

But we didn't move to Mandarin because Señor Estrada gave Ana Jai a present. We moved to Mandarin because of my half-brother Diego.

One evening, a long time ago, Martha told me what happened. We were catching zebra longwings, the black and white striped butterflies that flourish in La Florida in the summer when the purple passionflowers weave their way into the orange trees. Zebras sip the flower's nectar, which sends bunches of these butterflies into a trance.

We loved to push them onto our fingers without waking them. I once lined up fifteen zebras, a herd of them, on every finger of my left hand, and held 'em steady for seven minutes until one woke up and startled his friends into flight.

"You were only just born," said Martha, gently pushing a zebra off a flower and onto her forefinger. "Ana Jai heard another baby had been born to a Cuban woman named Isabel, whom Father had brought from Cuba. She was different from the rest. She wasn't African; she spoke Spanish. Ana Jai went to find out more. When she got to the cabin, she got the shock of her life. There was Father holding Isabel's newborn baby, just cooing at him and calling him 'my son Diego.' It made Ana Jai extremely jealous."

I know how jealousy feels. I used to feel that way when Father paid more attention to Martha than me. Those two could talk for hours about finding an appropriate husband for Martha. Father wanted him to be "gentry." That's what you call rich people in England, where Father is from. But Martha always said she couldn't meet any gentry living in the wilderness. That's what she called Mandarin.

Martha and Mary. Our names may begin with the same letter, but we are very different. She loves needlework and sits for hours cross-stitching sheep on pillowcases or the initials "ZK" on Father's handkerchiefs. I don't have the patience for that. I prefer the wilderness.

"Ana Jai did not talk to Father for days after she saw him with that baby," Martha said. "When she finally spoke, she said she was moving to Mandarin and taking us with her."

I studied several zebras sound asleep on a passion-flower.

"What was it like when Father lived with us?" I asked. That was a big question for me back then because I did not see Father much when we lived at Mandarin. I used to beg to spend more time with him.

"Ana Jai was happier. She smiled more," Martha sighed, as she remembered a time I couldn't recall. "Father seemed happier too. He didn't travel as much. We ate dinner together and talked about what we did that day."

It used to be that we'd only see Father several times a month, like when he crossed the St. Johns River to ride his white stallion, King Lear. He kept Lear on our side of the river because it was closer to St. Augustine.

Or we'd see him when he came to check on the trading store my brother George ran for him on Ana Jai's property. He also visited one Sunday a month when a traveling priest from St. Augustine said Mass in our barn. That was my favorite time to see Father. I liked to hold his hand and sit close to him during the service.

But when he was away on his sailing ship, we didn't see him for months.

"Do you think he'll ever live with us again?" I asked hopefully.

"Not unless Ana Jai allows it," said Martha, shaking her head. "And you know how often she changes her mind." Yep, I knew. Never.

I studied the school of butterflies asleep on my finger and wished my family could be together just like them.

"Come on, Mary," Martha said, interrupting my thoughts. "We need to get home."

And with that we each gave our hands a shake and sent a swirl of black and white stripes into the early evening light.

3

Ana Jai was not fond of Diego, but I sure was. We were the same age, the same height, and we loved to play the same games. Only difference: I could read. He could not.

Ana Jai wanted all her kids to learn reading so she hired "Tutor" a while back to teach us. That's what George called the old, spectacled man from England. Not "Mr. Barnwell" (his name) or "Sir," or even "Mr. Tutor." Just Tutor. Tutor didn't mind being called that, though, and he taught us to read *Aesop's Fables* before returning to England. I tried to teach Diego how to read the fables too, figuring he'd like all those ants and grasshoppers and such, but he wasn't interested.

"You do the reading," he said. "I'll listen."

Diego lived with his mother at Laurel Grove but crossed the river every day to take care of King Lear. Our general manager at Mandarin, Abraham Hanahan, a freed person who now worked for Ana Jai, used to take care of the stallion. But Abraham never liked him much. Abraham greatly preferred boats to horses. He used to work on Father's sailing ships. With his coal-black skin and silver hoop earring in one ear, Abraham looked a bit scary, like a pirate. But he wasn't scary at all, just quiet and strong.

In truth, Lear was a hard horse to like, high-strung and prone to kicking anyone who walked behind him, especially Abraham. But Diego always had a way with him. Father said Diego came by his horse-sense naturally: he inherited it from Father's father who lives in England.

I always wanted Diego to live with us at Mandarin, but Ana Jai would never hear of it, and besides, Diego didn't want to leave his mother at Laurel Grove.

So, most mornings, after breakfast, I waited for Diego on a long, wooden dock that poked out into the wide St. Johns River. Diego rowed across in a little boat to feed Lear, exercise him, and brush his coat. After that, we climbed a ladder to the Redbird Nest in the top of an old oak tree.

It was hard to spot the nest because it was hidden by gray Spanish moss dripping from the tree's limbs. Ana Jai had Abraham build it as a lookout, so we could keep an eye out for Patriots approaching in gunboats on the river. Ana Jai was not about to let herself be captured by those men. She called them thieves who wanted to steal our land and our Africans, and turn us back into slaves. And she swore she'd never be a slave again.

Me and Diego learned a long time ago to volunteer for lookout duty in the Redbird Nest. It was easy work and we never saw any Patriots. One morning, in particular, as we pushed through the door in the floor of the nest, we definitely were not thinking about Patriots.

"Panthers are the most dangerous animals in Florida," I said, shuffling a new deck of cards, a present from Father's recent trip to New York City. Panthers were on my mind because the night before I dreamed I was running through the woods on a sandy path. When I turned the corner on a thicket of palmetto bushes, I came eye to eye with a panther, same color as the path. It growled at me, showing its sharp, pointy teeth. Before I could run away, that panther grabbed me with its claws and sank its teeth into my leg.

Diego scoffed. I dealt the cards.

"Gators are by far the most dangerous animal in Florida. A gator will lock his jaws around your body and take you underwater forever. You'll drown before you ever get loose. Or it will roll over your body and crush your lungs. Or it will thrash its head from side to side while you're still in its jaws and tear—"

"Enough," I said. "You discard first."

As we played cards, our conversation resumed.

"Ana Jai is about as scared of snakes as she is of Patriots," I said. "She's afraid one will slither into her bed while she's asleep and sink its teeth into her. In Africa, she says snakes are as plentiful as hen's eggs."

That's why Ana Jai makes the Africans sweep the dirt around our house every night. It's powdery and fine because it's partly sand and when they're finished sweeping, the dirt looks smooth as fancy face powder. No one's allowed to touch it all night long because that would leave a print. First thing when she wakes up, Ana Jai walks around the outside porch looking for squiggly marks in the dirt. If she sees one, she clangs a big bell and the Africans come running. Then we all tear the house apart looking for snakes. We've never found a snake inside the house, but we did find one underneath it once. Ana Jai smashed it with a shovel.

A cool breeze blew through the fencing that surrounded the nest. I dove for the discard pile, trying to keep my new cards from blowing away. I waited for Diego to take his turn.

"Is that a sea cow?" I wondered aloud, looking between the fence slats at a big, grey lump floating in the water.

"Your turn," Diego said, holding down his discard so it wouldn't blow away.

"It looks kind of hairy," I said.

Diego turned to look then because normally a sea cow's back is smooth as a dolphin's.

"I think it's a person!" he shouted. Diego threw down his cards and turned to open the floor door.

"Wait for me," I cried, gathering the deck together, quick as I could. I shoved the cards into my dress pocket and followed Diego down the ladder.

We ran past the house, across the big yard and toward the dock. We ran past Martha, embroidering under a shady red cedar tree.

"What's going on?" she asked.

"Someone's drowning," I yelled, not bothering to stop and explain.

Out on the dock, we both hopped into Diego's boat. He rowed as fast as he could over to that person, who by now was spending a lot of time under water.

"It's an old man," I shouted from the front of the boat.

We waited until the man's gray head broke the surface again. He gasped for air.

"Here," I yelled, throwing him a line. The man reached for the rope with what looked like the last of his strength. I pulled him in. Diego joined me and soon as we could lay our hands on him, we each grabbed an underarm and yanked that man's skinny body up over the side of the boat.

He hung there, coughing up water, and managed to raise his head.

"La Florida?" he whispered?

"Yep, you made it," Diego answered.

We didn't say much as Diego rowed back to shore. Mostly the two of us tried not to stare at the raw, pink welts crisscrossing the man's backside from his shoulders to his waist. And the welts were infected too, because a thick, yellow liquid that looked like fresh cream oozed from the boils on his old, black back.

4

A greeting party waited for us on shore. Only it was an angry greeting party, not a friendly one. No one smiled, not George, Martha, Abraham Hanahan, nor the Africans gathered round the water's edge. And certainly not Ana Jai who stood right in the middle of everyone, hands on her hips, that familiar frown creasing her brow.

"A runaway," she declared as George and Abraham Hanahan waded into the water to gingerly unload him. Diego jumped out of the boat and pushed it ashore.

The African's legs were full of bug bites, his feet swollen and cut. George and Abraham laid him on his side underneath the shady red cedar.

"Can you talk?" Ana Jai asked, still frowning.

Either the African was feverish or just weighing his options because he did not answer. He only coughed up more water.

We stood there staring down at him, waiting to hear what Ana Jai wanted to do. "He cannot stay here," George said.

We all knew harboring a runaway slave from the United

States of America was like starting a fire in a dry grass field during a drought. It was a sure way to bring trouble to La Florida.

"He could stay at the cabins till he's well enough to move on," Abraham Hanahan offered.

Four cabins sat in a half-moon down the road from the main house. And just like the main house, the walls were made of palm tree logs, the roof of thatched palm fronds. Ana Jai's Africans lived in the cabins, which Ana Jai said reminded her of a smaller version of her Senegalese village.

"We don't know for sure if he's a runaway, he hasn't said anything yet," I said. Ana Jai fixed a stare on me that said I was so dumb I couldn't add one plus one.

Then she looked back at the pitiful African, and thought some more.

"He can stay until he's fit to leave," she announced. "Keep him out of sight. No one breathes a word of this to anyone, do you hear me?" She made that last remark looking directly at me and Diego.

"Yes, Ana Jai," I answered.

Diego looked down at the dirt, concentrating with all his might on burying an ant with his big toe.

"Yes, ma'am," he mumbled.

We knew Ana Jai didn't want us telling Father she was letting a runaway slave stay at Mandarin for a time. To be sure, this man's owners would come looking for him, and if they found him here, trouble would pound us like a hurricane.

"Martha, get the herb basket," she ordered.

Martha ran to the house to bring back the dried herbs she and Ana Jai used to brew terrible tasting teas and make smelly poultices whenever anyone was sick.

The herbs worked, though, and day by day the African

got better. He eventually told us his name, Gullah Jack. He was indeed a runaway from Georgia, where he'd been sold and beaten after his first master died. His first master was a large plantation owner in South Carolina and Gullah Jack was his manservant. He'd been his manservant ever since the master was a little boy. They grew up together, closer friends than the master would admit. Jack took care of a lot of business for him and consequently knew mathematics and reading, and the business of running a plantation. Gullah Jack was sold to pay some debts when this first master died. His second master, the one in Georgia, found Gullah Jack a bit too smart for his liking. He liked to break unruly slaves.

"I let him break me real quick," Gullah Jack said. "Then I took off, soon as I could."

Ana Jai wanted to make sure Gullah Jack stayed out of sight because a fair number of people came through Mandarin to trade at Father's store. She told him, real clear, he'd have to follow the rules if he wanted to stay awhile.

"You must not leave your cabin during daylight. When you're able, you can join the Seminoles," she said, speaking of the Native Americans who live deep in the swamps of La Florida and hate the Patriots as much as we do. They take in runaway slaves, because in truth, who else would live in the swamp if they didn't have to, with all those gators and snakes and mosquitoes about?

It wasn't long before we learned Gullah Jack could carve a piece of wood like nobody's business. Turns out he'd been carving ever since he was a boy, learned it from an old slave at his first plantation, who learned it in Africa.

Diego and I hauled pieces of driftwood up from the river bank and Gullah Jack set to making himself a stool to sit on. Once he had his stool, ole Jack never stopped carving. He made cooking spoons, big bowls, little bowls, broom handles, anything we wanted. All he needed was for someone to find him the wood 'cause he couldn't go looking for it himself.

George wanted to sell some of his things at the store but Ana Jai said no, someone may recognize his work.

Ana Jai wasn't so eager to see Gullah Jack go live with the Seminoles after she saw how useful his fingers could be.

"You must judge a man by the work of his hands," she said, reciting a proverb she remembered from Africa.

But she really softened on him when she learned he had another talent. Jack was a storyteller, just like her father the king had been in Senegal.

5

Ana Jai called him a conjurer. She said every good tribe in Africa had one.

The first story Gullah Jack ever conjured up for us was about an Indian chief named Coosawhatchie. He told it one night as he sat on his stool outside his cabin. Nighttime was the only time Ana Jai let Jack get fresh air. She figured the darkness hid him from prying eyes.

I can still see ole Jack carving a small piece of juniper wood, with all of us, including Ana Jai, gathered round. He designed his words like his carvings, slowly smoothing out a picture for all of us to hold.

He'd usually start carving by cutting the wood in half and resting one piece on the ground. Then he'd lay the other piece across his knee so he could smooth its edges. Then, he'd start conjuring.

"Coosawhatchie was a Creek from South Carolina. His hair was long, down past his shoulders, and shiny-black, like a raven's. He wore feathers for earrings, and a big silver medallion 'round his neck. He always wrapped a red kerchief 'round his head and tied it to one side, real handsome-like.

"If there was one thing Coosawhatchie hated it was having white folk living on his tribal land. He killed plenty of 'em and managed to avoid getting captured for years. But finally, as happens to most Indians, Coosawhatchie came down with a fever. It turned the whites of his eyes same color as summer squash."

Gullah Jack stopped talking to blow shavings out of a bowl he'd carved in the wood.

"Government soldiers caught him then 'cause he was so weak he couldn't run no more. They put him in a fort over in Charleston where a doctor tended to the fever. The doctor was fascinated by Coosawhatchie, gave him medicines and kept him alive long as he could, just to be near him. Then, one day, Coosawhatchie died. But the doctor didn't tell nobody, especially at the fort."

Gullah Jack shifted his attention now to the piece of juniper on the ground. He picked it up and held it to his nose, inhaling deeply.

"I just love the smell of juniper," he said. Then he began to carve this second piece of wood, smoothing out the sides.

"Instead, the doctor covered the Indian chief up to his neck with a blanket and told the soldiers not to touch him. He returned to town and got a big jar, about the size of that farm bell Ana Jai rings real loud when she wants everyone up at the main house. Then he put the jar in a box and brought it back to the fort. He went to Coosawhatchie's bedside and darned if he didn't chop the poor chief's head right off."

Gullah Jack stopped talking, and began digging out a little knob on the topside of the wood.

"The doctor stuffed Coosawhatchie's head into that

glass jar, put a lid on it, and placed the jar back in the box. He took the chief's pillow, folded it up and put it where the head used to be. He covered the chief's whole body, from pillow to toe, with a blanket so no one could tell he was stealing the poor man's head. Then he high-tailed it back to his office, where he put Coosawhatchie's head up on a shelf so he could look at him whenever he wanted."

"I don't believe that," George interrupted.

"Well, I seen it with my own two eyes when I went to town for the Missus. That chief still had his earrings on," Gullah Jack added.

George snorted, still disbelieving.

Gullah Jack stopped carving and placed the lid he'd just finished on top of the bowl he'd made earlier.

"Here, Ana Jai. A little jewelry box for you."

Ana Jai smiled and accepted the box, her thirteen bracelets chiming gently.

"Thank you, Jack," she said. She held the box up to her nose and inhaled deeply. "It's beautiful."

But truth be told, we were all a little stunned by Jack's story. And I don't think any of us, including Ana Jai, was completely sure whether it was true or not.

6

I've always been able to tell a lot about people by what they wear on their feet. I remember when Martha started wearing shoes every day. This was a big change for her since everyone ran around Mandarin barefoot, including Ana Jai. In fact, Diego and I refused to wear shoes until December and only then when it was good and cold out.

But Martha started wearing these little blue high heels Father bought her in New York City. If you ask me, she looked fairly silly tromping around the woods in high heels, but Martha said if she didn't wear shoes, she'd never get a husband. That's when Ana Jai would tell her, "Before you marry keep both eyes open. After you marry close one eye."

Martha rolled her eyes when she heard one of Ana Jai's proverbs, they irritated her so. Besides, she said, this proverb missed the point. She'd like to be choosy about a husband if there was anyone around to be choosy about, but out here in the wilderness, Martha insisted, the prospects of finding a husband were slim.

George showed signs of too much wilderness, too, and he wore shoes to prove it. They were black with square, silver buckles on top. Father bought them in Savannah and George wore them to show Father he was grown-up and responsible. George wanted to learn more about business from Father. He dreamed of leaving Mandarin on one of Father's trading ships. He wanted to see the world and make his fortune, maybe even attend boarding school in England. Ana Jai would hear nothing of this, however. She wanted to keep George and Martha and me by her side forever.

But George's growing pains showed up in another, more terrible, way: he refused to play with me and Diego anymore.

This made it impossible for us to enjoy our favorite game, "Ponce," in which we all pretended to be either Ponce de León or a member of his party, searching for the Fountain of Youth. That's what Tutor says the Spanish explorer was looking for when he landed in La Florida three hundred years ago.

Ole Ponce came ashore just south of here near St. Augustine, so we figure he may have stomped around our woods looking for that fountain, which Tutor says he never found. We haven't found it yet either, but searching for it sure can take up a day.

Anyway, George always took on the role of Ponce de León, but since he wouldn't play anymore, Diego and I couldn't play either. George mostly spent his days wearing shoes and running Father's store, which sat on a bluff above the river not far from Ana Jai's house. The store was just a cabin made from palm tree logs, but things got pretty busy there some days.

Families who lived nearby stopped at the store to buy

rum, which Father bought on his trips to Cuba, or salt for smoking pigs. Or they traded a bushel of pecans for, say, a bushel of Ana Jai's oranges.

Seminoles stopped there too, but they never had any money. They'd bring in a fresh-killed deer and, using sign language and grunts, let George know they wanted to trade it for a bag of corn meal or some other supplies.

"Keep them happy," Ana Jai once cautioned George. "We want the Seminoles to be our friends."

George's only hope of freedom was for Father to take him on a sailing trip. But so far, that had not happened— in part because Father was gone a lot himself. In fact, in December 1813 he was gone again on one of his ships, *La Ballena*, which means whale in Spanish. He left in September from the port of Fernandina. At the time, Father said he'd be back in two months, in time for Christmas, but depending on the seas and weather, we knew that would change.

Consequently, George was grumpy. His anger festered because Ana Jai refused to let him travel to the city of Fernandina to see Father off. She said it was too dangerous a place for a mulatto like George.

Fernandina is just north of us on Amelia Island, but we never go there. That's because it's spitting distance from Georgia, across the Cumberland Sound as the crow flies. Consequently, it's full of Patriots. A year ago, Patriots took control of Amelia Island and ran off a small detachment of Spanish soldiers stationed in Fernandina.

That was the first act in the Patriot's rebellion, which was designed to finish with the takeover of La Florida. For their second act, the Patriots needed to take over St. Augustine and for that they needed the help of the United States Army. But President James Madison wouldn't join the fight. He made the Patriots give Amelia Island back to Spain. That really made the Patriots mad. Ana Jai figures they're just waiting for another chance to get their grabby hands on La Florida.

"I told you, Mary, I don't have time to play that stupid game," George said, irritated that I kept begging him to play Ponce. Diego was smart. He let me do the begging while he sat atop of a bushel of pecans in the store, peeling an orange.

"Come on, George. It's a perfect day to search for the fountain."

"You should search for the buccaneers' treasure," said Gullah Jack, darting inside the store. He moved quiet and quick, like the lizards that darted across the path from the main house to the Africans' cabins.

Here was Jack, entering the store in broad daylight in direct defiance of Ana Jai's orders.

"What are you doing?" said George, shocked to see Jack in the daytime. "Someone might see you. Get back to the cabins."

"I need to sharpen my knife," Jack said. "Do you have a stone?"

George turned to a shelf behind him, grabbed a sharpening stone, and practically threw it at Gullah Jack.

"Take it back to your cabin. I'll get it later," George said.

Jack slipped the stone into his pocket and turned to go, but Diego stopped him.

"What buccaneers' treasure you talking about?" he asked.

"The one on Amelia," Jack replied.

"I've never heard of a buccaneers' treasure up on Amelia Island," George said, sounding considerably like he thought Gullah Jack was crazy.

"Well, there is one," Jack said simply.

Then he darted out the door like he darted in, leaving us to wonder just what in the world he was talking about.

7

George excused himself after dinner that evening, saying he had business to tend to at the cabins. I knew exactly what business he was talking about and followed as soon as the dishes were done. Although Ana Jai has Africans to do the housework, she doesn't want her children growing up lazy, so we all have chores. Dishwashing is mine.

I found George and Diego sitting on a log in front of Gullah Jack, who as usual, was whittling away.

"Fancy meeting you here," I said to Diego.

"Yep," he said, his eyes glittering. Diego smiled with his big dark eyes more than his mouth. It was just his way of keeping his emotions to himself.

But there was a problem. Gullah Jack didn't feel like telling us about the buccaneers' treasure. In fact, he didn't feel like talking, period.

"What kind of treasure is it?" George demanded.

"Dunno," said Jack.

"Where is it?" Diego asked.

"If I knew that I wouldn't be here now, would I," Jack snapped.

We all sat there, waiting for Gullah Jack to open up.

"Is a buccaneer same as a pirate?" I asked, hoping to get Jack started on the conjuring.

He looked up from his whittling, staring at me for a moment. Then he looked back down and slowly started talking.

"Nope. Big difference. Pirates work for themselves. They fly a black flag on their ship with a white skull and crossbones on it. Anyone sees that flag knows to beware 'cause there's pirates aboard. A pirate will cut your throat faster than a hummingbird can beat its wings.

"Buccaneers are nicer. They work for a country and fly that country's flag on their ship. Whatever treasure they get, they turn it over to that country and keep a little, a percentage, for themselves."

Jack had our full attention now and he knew it. He paused for dramatic effect, making us wait for details.

"Fifty years ago, a buccaneer ship dropped anchor at Fernandina, flying the flag of England. The buccaneers raided a Spanish galleon full of gold and emeralds from Mexico. But they had no intention of turning the bulk of this gold over to the king of England. Instead, they planned to give the king just a little, and keep most of it for themselves."

"So they were really pirates?" I asked.

He looked at me and smiled. "I guess. They buried most of the gold doubloons and emerald jewelry on Amelia Island until they could return for it. And they set out for England to give the king a small percentage of their treasure. Trouble is, their ship sank in a storm, and they all drowned."

"How do you know this?" George asked, suspicious that Gullah Jack was making this up.

"Before they left, a buccaneer gave directions to the treasure to his girlfriend, a freed negro, to hold onto. It was all put down on a piece of leather. The girl didn't know what it said for years. She couldn't read."

"And what did it say?" George asked.

"It said the treasure was buried underneath a giant oak on Amelia Island. The buccaneers hung a chain from a branch of that tree, dangled it right above the treasure. They figured the chain would help 'em find it again someday."

"Did she dig it up once she could read?" I asked.

"She tried to, but a big storm changed the area, real good. Knocked down trees and branches. She couldn't find anything."

"I don't believe you," said George.

Gullah Jack paused in his whittling and uttered his next two sentences with more strength and conviction then I'd ever heard come out of that little man.

"I seen those directions with my own two eyes. That freed negro woman lives in Charleston now. Keeps the leather in a pouch tied 'round her neck."

"So the treasure is still out there?" Diego asked.

"I expect," Jack said, returning to his whittling.

"Did the directions tell how to find the tree?" I wanted to know.

"It said take the main road east from Fernandina to Sadler's Creek. When you get to the creek, walk north five hundred paces. Then look for a big oak tree with a chain hanging down."

"Is the chain still there?" George asked.

"Don't know. I expect that's part of the problem." Jack

said. "No one can find the right tree."

We all just sat there watching Jack whittle and thinking private thoughts about the treasure.

And in the days ahead, George, Diego, and I each came down with a powerful case of gold fever. But, Martha, once we told her the story, did not catch the fever at all. In fact, she called Gullah Jack's story "silly."

8

From the moment Gullah Jack told us of the treasure, we wanted to search for it. But we couldn't. Ana Jai would never allow George or me to leave Mandarin and travel to Amelia Island to dig for gold doubloons and emerald jewelry. We didn't even bother asking. Diego could have gone—his mother let him do what he wanted. But even he knew it was too long a journey to make alone.

We thought about sneaking away, but going north to Amelia Island took half a day by boat. Then we still had to find Sadler's Creek and the oak tree and dig. There was no way we could accomplish all that and return to Mandarin without Ana Jai finding out.

There was nothing to do but wait. But remarkably, we didn't have to wait long.

Several weeks after Gullah Jack told us the treasure story, a merchant knocked at our door selling wares. It was helpful to have these merchants stop by because they sold things we needed but couldn't make ourselves, things like paper, books, and embroidery needles.

They also brought news.

"Get me the lady of the house," the man demanded when I answered the door. He wasn't a very handsome man, with wild gray hair that buzzed around his head like a pack of horseflies.

"Yes, sir," I said, smiling to myself because I knew what was coming next.

I found Ana Jai seated at a table working on receipts.

"There's a merchant here."

"Good," she replied. Ana Jai stood up, pulled herself tall, her head held high. She walked to the door like the finest African princess you've ever seen. I was right on her heels, not wanting to miss a thing.

"Yes?" she said to the merchant, who had opened his haversack and was setting up a display of his wares on the front porch, a display that included some very pretty hair ribbons, I might add. The man looked up.

"I told that little mulatto I wanted the lady of the house," he said sharply.

"That's me," Ana Jai replied, frosty as a winter morning. She folded her hands at her waist and waited.

The man stared at my mother, his mouth registering surprise. He looked at me and then he looked back at Ana Jai. During those brief seconds, the man figured out he'd have to be nice to this African woman if he wanted to make a sale. And since he was, no doubt, a practical man with a very heavy haversack, he softened his tone.

"Pardon," he mumbled, looking away.

"Do you have any ledgers?" Ana Jai asked, looking over his wares.

The man pulled two ledger books from the bottom of his sack.

"One dollar. Each," he said, defiantly, looking straight at Ana Jai.

That was a high price, we both knew. But the fact that he asked to be paid in dollars, the official currency of the United States of America, and not in Spanish coins, the official currency of La Florida, was worrisome. We didn't say anything, but I knew Ana Jai was wondering same as me, was this man really a merchant or a Patriot spy from Georgia sent to investigate our plantation?

"Choose some hair ribbons, Mary."

Now that was music to my ears. Much to this merchant's irritation, I fingered every last one of his hair ribbons before deciding on a lovely blue one, edged in white lace, for Martha. It would match her eyes. I picked an apple green one for me because green's my favorite color.

"Any peppermint sticks?" Ana Jai asked, for she had a sweet tooth far worse than any of her children.

The man grunted and pulled out a sack full.

"How much for everything?" she asked.

"Two dollars. American," the man said, just itching for a fight.

Ana Jai remained imperious.

"Mary, run and get my money pouch," she said.

"What news have you?" she asked the merchant as I went inside. I could hear their conversation through an open window, but I rushed to return with the pouch, not wanting to miss a thing.

"Patriots attacked the Fatio plantation."

"What?" said Ana Jai, her face registering surprise. Francis Philip Fatio was a longtime friend of Father's. He owned a large plantation some ten miles away from us. "When did this happen?"

"Last week," said the merchant, proud to be telling Ana

Jai this shocking news. Then I wondered, was this merchant really proud to be telling Ana Jai the news, or proud Patriots attacked the Fatio plantation?

"Fatio, his family, and some of his slaves escaped by boat, but Patriots captured forty of his Negroes. Last I heard they were taking them up to Savannah to put them on the auction block."

This news sent a shock wave through me, as it must have to Ana Jai. Still, neither of us showed any emotion.

"What about the Spanish?" Ana Jai asked.

"They're too afraid to leave their fort in St. Augustine. Conquistadors, ha!" he said, spitting a wad of saliva on the ground. "Mark my words, missy. East Florida will be free of the king of Spain any day now."

Ana Jai opened her money pouch to pay this man and send him on his way.

She handed him a gold bit, a slice of a Spanish gold coin that had been cut into eight pieces. It was worth far more than two dollars, the merchant knew.

He snatched it out of Ana Jai's hand. The gold disappeared into his pocket.

"Sure is a nice place you got here," he said, eyeing Ana Jai's house and looking around the yard as he packed up his wares. "This all belong to you?"

"Yes," she said.

Then, just like Gullah Jack did when he was conjuring, Ana Jai paused for dramatic emphasis. She said her next sentence slow and strong.

"We are loyal to the crown."

I'll say one thing for Ana Jai, she wasn't going to let this merchant or Patriot or whatever he was push her around. She drew her line in the sand and as much as told him so by admitting her loyalty to the king.

The merchant stuffed the last of his wares into his sack and hoisted it to his shoulder. He was ready to walk to the next plantation, or back to Georgia if that's where he came from. But he was determined to get the last word in before he left.

"Remember this, little missy," he said, as an odd smile crossed his bright red face. "Your king will be far away in Spain when the Patriots come a-calling."

"Get out," Ana Jai said, spitting her words at him like Seminole arrows.

The man turned and walked away, whistling a tuneless song.

Ana Jai quietly told me to fetch George, Martha, and Abraham Hanahan. "Hurry," she said before the merchant even left the yard. "We must act quickly."

9

We found Ana Jai pacing the floor of the main house, her arms crossed tightly at her chest.

She gave no greeting.

"Patriots attacked Señor Fatio's plantation last week. Mandarin could be next. I'm going to St. Augustine to beg the governor for soldiers to protect us."

"I'll go with you," George offered.

"No, I need you to stay here and watch Mandarin. Martha, pack up the house; George pack up the store. Put everything in the cotton baskets and hide them in the woods near the oyster mounds."

The oyster mounds stuck out of the woods like sand dunes. They were leftover from the Shell People, Native Americans who lived here a long time ago and ate oysters morning, noon, and night, which is simply amazing to me because I think eating an oyster is like eating a slug. Anyway, the Shell People threw every oyster shell they ever ate into a pile, creating lots of big hills, some at least ten feet tall.

Ana Jai issued more orders.

"Mary, sit in the Redbird Nest. If you see anything suspicious, warn everyone. Hide in the woods if necessary. All of you, stay together. The oyster mounds will be our meeting place if you're not here when I get back."

She turned her attention to Abraham Hanahan.

"Abraham, get the boat ready. We'll leave in an hour and return in two days."

Abraham nodded and left the room. Father called him the best riverboat pilot on the St. Johns River. He'd get them to St. Augustine and back safely.

Ana Jai stopped pacing and looked out a window across the river to Father's plantation.

"Mary, make sure you tell Diego about the Patriots. He can warn Laurel Grove," she said.

"Yes, Ana Jai."

"Go. Everyone. There's much to do."

As always, whenever Father was gone, I wished he were home. But this time as I ran to the Redbird Nest for lookout duty, I didn't just miss Father. I feared for our future. I knew we'd be much safer if he were about.

Even with the threat of Patriots closing in on us, I couldn't help noticing the view from the Redbird Nest. The only movement on the St. Johns River came from a pair of ospreys diving into the water to catch fish. Laurel Grove seemed quiet too, at least the part of it I could see through the trees along the riverbank.

I set out a signal flag for Diego and waited for him to row across the river. Long ago, we agreed if I ever needed to tell him anything important, I'd hang a red cloth on a certain branch near the Redbird Nest. He could see that branch from the other side of the river in Laurel Grove.

I watched Ana Jai and Abraham Hanahan sail off until

their boat disappeared round a bend. They had to pass Señor Fatio's plantation in order to get to St. Augustine and they planned to do that at night, with darkness covering them like a blanket as they sailed by.

"Be careful, Ana Jai," I whispered.

Before long, Diego rowed across the river and ran to the nest.

"What's the matter?" he said, climbing through the floor door.

Diego frowned when I told him about Señor Fatio's plantation and Ana Jai's departure to St. Augustine.

"If they attack Mandarin, they'll attack Laurel Grove," he said when I finished.

"That's what Ana Jai thinks. She wants you to warn everyone over there."

"If Ana Jai returns with Spanish soldiers it will be safer over here," said Diego.

I nodded, sensing what was coming.

"I'm bringing my mother over," he said.

"Diego, you can't bring Isabel here. Ana Jai will be furious."

"I don't care. I can't let anything happen to her, Mary. She's my mother. I'll hide her in the barn. Besides, if I'm over here, I can help fight the Patriots if they come."

His mind was made up.

"When is Ana Jai returning?" he asked.

"In two days."

"I'm bringing Isabel over here tomorrow."

As I watched him climb down from the Redbird Nest and row back to Laurel Grove, I thought that life sure can take you by surprise. With Ana Jai gone to St. Augustine, we could have sneaked away to hunt for the buccaneers' treasure. Instead we had to prepare for a possible fight with the Patriots.

10

There's not much to do when you're on watch duty in the Redbird Nest. I took short naps, sang, played cards with myself, that sort of thing. I also watched a pair of fat redbirds add straw to their own nest above me in the tree.

Still, by the time darkness fell on the second day, I was dog-tired from sitting around doing nothing. Thus, I was greatly relieved when George climbed up to spell me for the night.

"Get some sleep," he said.

I took my weary bones to bed, curling up next to Martha, who was already asleep in the house.

Next thing I knew, Ana Jai shook me awake.

"Get up, Mary," she said. "Get your sister up."

"You're home," I mumbled, half asleep, but not too asleep to notice it was still dark out.

"Meet me in the yard. Quickly."

I woke up Martha, which in truth was not easy. As she stumbled out of bed, I pulled on my dress and ran to the yard.

I was surprised to see a large assembly already there. All the

Africans, including Gullah Jack, stood around Ana Jai. She held a pile of papers in her arms. Abraham Hanahan stood at her side, a bright, burning torch in his hand. George must have seen them arrive from the Redbird Nest because he was on the other side of Ana Jai, holding a torch, too. Diego joined me. He must have left Laurel Grove with his mother. Martha arrived a moment later, squeezing her way up front so as not to miss anything.

Ana Jai addressed the crowd.

"The other night, as we sailed to St. Augustine, we passed Señor Fatio's plantation. I looked ashore to see something I never want to see again: Patriot campfires burning in the Fatios' yard. I smelled the Patriots' food, watched them walk in and out of Señor Fatio's home." She paused a moment for emphasis. "I will *never* allow this to happen at Mandarin."

I wanted to cry out, ask how she could prevent it, but dared not interrupt.

"The governor of La Florida sent me back here with five soldiers. They're in a gunboat over at the dock right now."

Five soldiers, I thought to myself. That's not enough to protect us from a Patriot attack. We need fifty-five soldiers, or 105, and cannons and gunpowder.

"They are not here to fight," Ana Jai continued. "They are here to help us flee."

She paused, taking a deep breath.

I think Ana Jai might have been the only one breathing at this point because the rest of us froze in anticipation, waiting for what she'd say next.

"I have freedom papers for all my Africans."

She waved the pile of papers in the air.

"I wrote one for each of you as we sailed back from St. Augustine. These papers include your original bill of sale.

You can go where you will with them, but I suggest you take great pains to hide from any Patriots. They'd just as soon tear up these papers and ship you to a slave auction in Georgia."

Ana Jai proceeded to call the names of each of her Africans, handing them his or her papers.

When she got to the end of her stack, she called one more name.

"Gullah Jack," she said, handing the last piece of paper to him.

"You're not mine to free, Jack, but I wrote this for you just the same. If anyone gives you trouble, show this. It says you were freed by me on this day, December seventeenth, eighteen-thirteen."

Gullah Jack stared at the paper. It trembled slightly in his hands.

"Thank you," he said quietly.

"Now, I can't tell you where to go or what to do," she told the crowd. "But I suggest you get on the governor's gunboat and head south to St. Augustine. You'll be safe there. Remember, you're free now."

The Africans were stunned. No one moved, really; this was all so sudden. Gullah Jack interrupted the awkward silence.

"Where are *you* going?" he asked.

We all stood there, waiting to hear Ana Jai's answer.

"Abraham Hanahan is taking us north to the port of Fernandina on Amelia Island. We're leaving by boat in one hour."

"Fernandina?" Martha cried out. "But that's next to Georgia, closer to the Patriots!"

"I know," Ana Jai replied calmly. "But one does not wander far from where the corn is roasting."

"What's that supposed to mean?" Martha demanded.

"Spain still controls Fernandina and La Florida," said Ana Jai. "I realize there are Patriots there, but there are Patriots here, too. Your father's ship will dock in Fernandina when he returns. He is our best protection."

She said that last part kind of quiet. I wondered why she was including Father in her reasoning since she usually took care of things herself. But I guess even Ana Jai, strong as she was, knew when she needed help.

"Get your belongings," Ana Jai ordered. "The boats leave in fifteen minutes."

Fifteen minutes! That was barely enough time to grab some clothes.

As the crowd broke up I found Diego. "What will you do?" I asked, fearful for his future.

"Go with you to Amelia Island."

"But Ana Jai won't let you."

"Yes, she will. Meet me in the barn in five minutes. Hurry."

I ran to the main house to get my clothes, my cards, and a palm frond sun hat. That was about all that was left in our room anyway since Martha had packed everything up. Then I ran to the barn because I figured Diego had some plan in mind, even though I couldn't imagine what it was.

11

Ifound Diego tightening a black leather saddle around King
Lear's belly. The saddle, with its silver adornments, was a gift
to Father from Governor Estrada.

"What are you doing? There's no time to ride Lear."

Isabel stood quietly outside Lear's stall, nervously fingering
a large square of cloth. I could hear yelling outside the barn and
I imagined everyone gathering their things and running for the
gunboats.

Diego adjusted a bit in the horse's mouth.

"I can't leave him," he said.

"Well you can't ride him anywhere either. The woods are
full of Patriots."

I looked to Isabel to agree with me on this.

She said nothing, just nervously fingered the cloth. The
barn began to smell like smoke. There must be a fire somewhere, I thought.

"I'm not riding him," said Diego. "I'm putting him on the
riverboat to Fernandina." He held out his hand. Isabel handed

him the cloth, which Diego folded in half, into a triangle.

"Father would never forgive me if I left Lear behind. Patriots would ride him to death. Or Seminoles might eat him for supper."

Both were distinct possibilities.

Diego whispered in Lear's ear, talking softly so only the horse could hear him. He held the cloth in front of Lear's nose and slowly brought it up to cover the horse's eyes, which by now looked a little wild. He tied the cloth around Lear's head, clucking softly in a special, reassuring language only the two of them understood.

"Let's go," Diego said, leading Lear out of his stall.

As we walked toward the barn doors, I stopped short, dumbfounded when I saw what was happening in the yard. Our house was on fire and Ana Jai was setting the flames.

King Lear smelled the smoke and started to rear up. Diego, however, pulled him down and patted his neck, whispering in the horse's ear to calm him.

My mother, meanwhile, touched a torch to a corner of our roof and held it there until flames licked the dry palm fronds. They crackled as they burned like a rattlesnake's rattle. Then Ana Jai ran to the other end of the house and touched her torch to the roof again. Flames consumed this end, working their way toward the middle. Smoke filled the night air like fog from the river. The bitter smell of burning palm fronds gave me a sudden headache.

I knew this was really happening, but it felt like a dream, a dream that wasn't over yet. Ana Jai heaved her torch high into the middle of the roof. It landed with a thud. Smoke rose up almost immediately. In short order, three separate roof fires grew into one big blaze. And in the bright firelight I watched Ana Jai step back and take full measure of her work. She seemed oddly pleased to see her proud home go up in flames. I could not comprehend why she'd done such a thing.

George ran past the barn, interrupting my dream.

"Get on the boat," he yelled.

As he ran by, I turned to see the cabins, Ana Jai's little African village, totally engulfed in flames. Mandarin was no longer a quiet plantation. It was an inferno that would take months or years to rebuild.

"Come on," Diego said. He pulled Lear out of the barn and into the yard. Isabel gently put her arm around me and I stumbled forward. All the while Diego patted Lear's neck, whispering reassurances in the horse's ear. I was surely grateful Lear could not see this mayhem. No doubt it would have spooked him good.

Diego led the horse onto the dock. His hoofs echoed heavily on the wooden planks. I feared the wood might crack under the horse's weight, sending us all into the river. We passed the Spanish gunboat, already packed with Ana Jai's Africans.

Diego walked straight ahead toward the end of the dock where Ana Jai's riverboat was tied up. I held my breath. Without stopping, Diego walked Lear down a wide plank that served as a bridge onto the boat. He never gave the horse a chance to balk, all the time whispering sweet nothings in its ear. He stepped aboard and pulled Lear onto the boat after him. The horse clomped around uneasily; the boat swayed back and forth. I worried the horse's weight might sink it. But Diego offered Lear a stick of sugar cane from his back pocket and the horse settled down, chewing happily. Still, Diego kept the kerchief over Lear's eyes, fearful the horse might spook.

I climbed aboard and so did Isabel. There the four of us stood, waiting to leave. Moments later, Martha walked down the dock, carrying a basket of oranges. A smaller basket containing her sewing things was nestled carefully in the middle of the sweet-smelling fruits.

George followed close behind Martha. He threw his torch into the water. It hissed like a snake as the flame went out.

Abraham came last, looking anxious.

They all stopped short and froze when they saw us aboard the back of the boat. Then Abraham simply walked around George and Martha and climbed aboard. My brother and sister followed. No one said one word, for in truth, the only words that mattered were to come.

Ana Jai approached soon after. She bid a fond farewell to the Spanish gunboat.

"¡*Ten cuidado!* Be careful!" she called, oddly cheerful for someone whose house was burning to the ground. Ana Jai waved to the departing soldiers and her newly freed Africans. Then she turned to see her boat, filled to the gills with all of us, including a horse. But Ana Jai did not skip a beat. She did not acknowledge Lear, Diego, or Isabel. But she did not order them off either.

Instead, she walked down the plank, forever the proud African princess, and ordered Abraham Hanahan to get going.

Abraham nudged his way around King Lear and got to work at the back of the boat. He unfastened a long pole tied to the boat's side and dug the pole into the river bottom. Then he pushed the stick with all his might to move the boat away from shore. George did the same thing and before long we were in the middle of the river. Abraham raised the riverboat's single sail and we waited for it to fill with wind.

Tears, meanwhile, filled my eyes as I watched the only

home I had ever known dissolve in smoke and flames.

"Ana Jai?" I said, standing next to her. We watched a roof beam fall to the ground in a shower of sparks.

"Yes?"

"Why did you burn the house down?"

"Mary, I would rather lose *everything* I own than give *any* of it to the Patriots."

I did not agree. Right now those flames seared a hole in my heart. And the Redbird Nest! Would it burn too? Tears poured from my eyes. I wiped them away with the sleeve of my dress.

George and Martha hardly seemed to care. George helped Abraham with the boat and Martha fussed with her sewing basket.

The riverboat's sail filled with a light morning breeze, and as it did I wondered if we were leaving one disaster, only to head into another.

12

We docked in Fernandina that afternoon. Ana Jai wanted everyone to see us arrive. She figured it was better to announce our arrival then to try and sneak into town when it was dark. And, Ana Jai said Father would have an easier time finding us if more people knew where we were.

Fernandina was named in honor of King Ferdinand VII, Prince of Spain. It was such a different place from our quiet plantation in the woods! Ships from all over the world came to this port town and moored in the harbor. Sailors used small boats to unload cargo and bring it ashore, things like tea from England, spices from the Bahamas, even slaves from Africa.

One dusty street, Centre Street, led in and out of the waterfront, and when a big ship arrived, wagons crowded the street like honeybees in a hive.

Ale houses, restaurants, and shops lined both sides of Centre Street. One store sold house wares, another quills, ink, and paper, and yet another, an apothecary, sold medicines. It was all very exciting.

We must have been quite a sight: two very dark Africans, one Cuban lady, three mulattos, one half-Cuban, and a big white horse all parading up Centre Street. Folks came out of their shops just to look at us. Ana Jai led the way and we all followed, carrying our small sacks of belongings. George now carried the basket of oranges because Martha said it was too heavy.

"Why are we bringing these anyway?" George grumbled.

"I will plant the seeds at my new home," Ana Jai replied. George rolled his eyes and tried to shift the burdensome basket to a more comfortable position in his arms.

Halfway down the street, Ana Jai stopped next to a wagon. Its African driver had been staring at us as we approached. The look on his face betrayed the same mix of fear and pride I often felt about my mother.

"Excuse me," Ana Jai said.

"Yessum?" the man said.

"Do you know where Captain Clarke lives?"

"Right over there." The African pointed to a large wooden house with a wraparound porch just off Centre Street. Sprigs of green holly, dotted with red berries, decorated the windows and doorway for Christmas.

"Thank you," said Ana Jai. She turned and marched toward the house. We dutifully followed.

Captain Clarke is Father's business partner. Together the two operate sailing ships with all-African sailing crews, which is different from other sailing ships and a point of pride for my father. Abraham used to sail for Father, which is why Father put so much trust in his abilities on the water.

"Wait here," Ana Jai ordered. She left us by the street to knock on Captain Clarke's front door. An African woman answered and spoke with Ana Jai for several seconds. Ana Jai returned to us, smiling.

"Captain Clarke is on *La Ballena* with Zephaniah. We can stay at his house until they both return."

"What about Diego?" I asked immediately. Ana Jai was still pretending Diego and his mother were not with us.

"There's a stable out back for Lear and for those accompanying him. Now I'm going inside for a cup of tea."

Ana Jai turned on her heel and walked back to the house.

I looked at Diego and smiled. Ana Jai would not acknowledge him or his mother, but she had secured them both a place to stay.

Together Diego and I walked Lear to the barn. His mother followed.

Diego jabbed his elbow into my side.

"Now we can search for the treasure," he whispered.

In the rush to leave Mandarin I did not realize we were now exactly where we wanted to be: on Amelia Island, the very same island where buccaneers buried gold coins and emerald jewelry that would make us rich beyond our wildest dreams.

13

Diego wanted to search for the treasure that very night. I, on the other hand, had no burning desire to go out in the woods in an area known to be full of Patriots. I also wanted George to come with us, but Diego did not. He thought George might tell Ana Jai what we were doing. Diego also thought it best to ride Lear when we went to search for the treasure. I disagreed, because I was sure Lear would awaken Isabel when we took him out of the barn.

In the end, we agreed to wait a few days and think about the best way to proceed. We also needed to find out exactly how to get to Sadler's Creek, a key landmark in Gullah Jack's directions.

Meantime, Ana Jai would not let us go outdoors, fearing we'd be kidnapped by Patriots. She kept George, Martha, and me inside Captain Clarke's house, the curtains closed tight, the doors locked.

This made George angry as a cut snake. He didn't like being locked up. And, truth be told, I was angry, too. I still didn't understand why Ana Jai burned down the house, and I secretly hoped Father would be angry at her when he found out what she had done.

"When will Zephaniah return?" Ana Jai worried aloud at the breakfast table the morning after we arrived.

"If you'd let me out of this house I could go watch for his ship at the docks. I'm not a slave you can order around, you know," George hissed.

Ana Jai blinked, surprised at George's strike.

She must have thought about what he said, because that evening as we ate biscuits and molasses for dinner, George frowning all the while at his food, Ana Jai made an announcement.

"George, I want you to spend your days at the docks watching for Father's ship. We must stop him before he goes to Laurel Grove."

"Good," said George.

"Check in during the day so I know what's going on," Ana Jai added.

George's freedom made Martha and me all the more antsy. Martha figured if George was allowed to go out then Ana Jai should let us out, too. Martha seemed to be past her fear of Patriots now that there were shops to visit in Fernandina.

"I'll take Mary with me," Martha begged.

After a day of pleading, Ana Jai relented and allowed us to leave the house too, but we had to promise to return in an hour.

"If you do not return in time, I will send Abraham Hanahan to find you and you will not be allowed out again," she said.

I had no intention of visiting shops with my precious time outdoors and informed Martha of this as soon as we stepped off the front porch. However, she insisted we stay together and made me agree to shop with her for thirty minutes. Then we'd spend our remaining thirty minutes at the docks with George.

We visited a dry goods store and Martha selected some fine embroidery thread. I chewed strings of black licorice purchased from the shopkeeper.

Afterward, we walked down Centre Street toward the docks looking for our brother. He wasn't hard to find, sitting on a bale of cotton talking to Diego. I felt left out seeing the two of them conversing without me.

"Do you know what tonight is?" Diego asked after we said our hellos.

"The eve of the eve of Christmas," said Martha.

"No," said Diego.

"Two days before my birthday," I tried.

"No," said Diego.

"What, then?" asked George.

"A full moon," Diego answered. "It's a perfect night to search for the treasure."

I swallowed hard.

"What treasure?" Martha asked.

Diego told her the same story Gullah Jack told us about the buccaneer bounty. Martha started laughing before Diego even finished.

"That's the silliest thing I've ever heard," she said. "There's no buccaneer treasure buried on Amelia Island."

"How do you know?" Diego countered.

"It can't hurt to just look for it, Martha," George said.

"And how do you expect to do that?" she asked.

"We'll search tonight while the moon's bright enough to guide us. We can ride out on Lear and be back before anyone even knows we're gone," Diego replied.

"Sneak out of the house! When Ana Jai finds out she'll beat you till kingdom come. Even you, Diego."

That gave me pause, for Ana Jai did not hold back when it came to punishment. Still, Diego was determined to search for the treasure. And George, feeling defiant, was determined to loosen the grip Ana Jai held on his life. They both agreed to set out this night in search of the buccaneer's bounty.

"I'm going, too," I declared.

"No," said George. "Only two people can ride Lear. Anyway it's too dangerous."

Martha interrupted. "If you don't let her go, I'll tell Ana Jai," she said.

My eyes met Martha's. She flashed me a quick, knowing look. I loved her more than ever at that moment because of her support, even if she didn't believe in what I wanted to do.

"Oh, fine," Diego said. "George and I can take turns walking while Mary rides Lear."

Martha did not realize it then, but she had just put herself in a very complicated position. She had no desire to hunt for the treasure, but she didn't try to stop us or tell Ana Jai about our plans.

Martha had no way of knowing she'd soon be in just as much trouble as the rest of us.

14

From our room in the second floor of Captain Clarke's house, George and I looked down into the backyard to see Diego and King Lear waiting for us. The white stallion gleamed in the moonlight.

I followed George down each creaky stair—there were thirteen altogether—and we managed to get outside without anyone, especially Ana Jai, coming after us. Diego greeted us silently, holding the reins to King Lear's bridle in one hand, two shovels from the good captain's barn in the other.

"Here," he whispered, handing the shovels to George.

Diego tucked the reins under his arm and cupped his hands together.

"Climb up," he whispered to me.

I've been on King Lear before and didn't like it much, but this was no time to complain. I stepped into Diego's cupped hands and he lifted me into the saddle. He held onto the reins and lead Lear out of the yard. With one hand, I gathered my cloak tightly around my neck, protection from the nighttime chill. With the other, I grabbed Lear's mane and held on. George sprinted ahead to lead the way, a shovel resting on each shoulder.

We headed west, away from Centre Street, toward the Old Cobb Road. Folks at the dock had told George it led to Sadler's Creek.

The full moon lit up our path like a lantern, just as Diego said it would. I could even see my breath filling the air in front of me with puffs of smoke. Nothing moved. Not even a dog barked, probably because most animals were holed up somewhere warm, refusing to move. We said little, fearing we'd draw attention to ourselves.

By the time we reached Sadler's Creek, the road narrowed. We no longer passed fields or fenced-in farms, just thick stands of palmetto, pine, and palm trees, along with occasional oaks. We paused at the creek, uncertain what to do next.

"Here's where we turn north and walk five hundred paces," Diego said. He turned left, pulling Lear along behind him. Diego walked in giant steps parallel to the creek, counting each step out loud. George followed behind us.

"One. Two. Three. Four. Five," Diego said.

"Diego, what if your steps are too small," I cried from my perch atop Lear.

"Ten. Eleven. Twelve," was his only reply.

"Don't worry, Mary. We'll figure it out," George said.

The shores of the creek rose and fell with the vagaries of the landscape. Sometimes we were on high ground, sometimes we were right next to the water.

"One hundred and one. One hundred and two. One hundred and three."

"Can I walk?" I asked, eager to do something besides ride Lear.

"Stay there," said George, not wanting to interrupt Diego.

At step 456 we entered a grove of oak trees sitting on a low rise above the creek.

At exactly five hundred paces we stopped near a grand old oak. Long strands of Spanish moss hung from the tree like the tangled hair of an old witch. The only thing missing from this tree was a chain hanging down to mark the treasure's burial spot.

I slid off Lear. "Now what?" I asked.

"We dig," said George.

"Where?" I replied.

"Anywhere," said Diego, looking up at a long, crusty limb covered with ferns.

"I'll start here," he said, planting his shovel in the ground directly underneath. *Crunch.* His shovel dug into the earth.

"I'll work over here," said George, heading to the other end of the great oak. He had his eye on another long limb, which hung over Sadler's Creek. This limb seemed to point toward the marsh like Gullah Jack's craggy finger, pointing toward the treasure.

"I want to dig, too," I complained.

Diego grunted, too busy to talk, and I knew I'd have to wait my turn.

The tree's trunk was so big it could have been three oak trees combined. I looked up, high into its branches, and strained to see any signs of a chain outlined in the moonlight. I thought if the chain wasn't hanging anymore, maybe it had worn a scar into the bark. I searched for signs of this while waiting for Diego to share the shovel, but found nothing.

Diego, meanwhile, dug a small channel some six inches

deep the length of the tree limb above.

"Think you're digging deep enough?" I asked.

"I don't know," he replied. "But I figured . . ."

"Help!" A voice called from the distance.

"George!" I cried, fear running through me. I ran toward the creek, Diego at my heels. We found George lying on the bank, near the water. A long, dark log lay beside him. Nothing moved, especially my brother.

We scurried down to help, stopping short. What looked like a log from the bluff above turned out to be a very long alligator, its mouth clamped firmly around George's left ankle.

"Diego, do something," I cried.

Diego was already moving. He grabbed George's shovel and bashed that gator on its head. Then he bashed it again and was about to bash it a third time when the gator released its hold on George and slipped across the creek, disappearing into the tall marsh grass.

"George," I cried, rushing toward him.

"My foot," he said.

"I'll get Lear," said Diego, running back up the bank. I lifted George's head and rested it on my lap.

"Musta' been a female. Musta' got too close to her nest," he said softly, sucking in air and wincing as he tried to move his foot.

Diego arrived with Lear. We stood George up on his one good foot. His other foot, the one the gator nearly chomped off, dangled close to the ground. Blood dripped out of holes in George's boot, holes put there by the gator's teeth.

We hoisted George into the saddle and started back to Captain Clarke's house, back, of course, to Ana Jai.

15

It took forever to get back to Fernandina. The gator bit straight through shoe leather and George was bleeding badly. Diego took the boot off and tied a kerchief around George's ankle, but it did little to stem the flow of blood. It wasn't long before Diego's kerchief became a dark, wet rag.

George didn't say much, just clung to the saddle as we headed back to Fernandina, fast as possible. But he got weaker as the ride got longer till finally he slumped forward and almost fell off the horse. That's when Diego determined I should ride Lear too, sitting in front of George so my brother could cling to me. In this manner we finally got home.

The roosters in Captain Clarke's chicken coop crowed their early morning greeting as we dragged George, his arms across each of our shoulders, up the front porch steps.

I banged on the front door repeatedly until Ana Jai finally peeked through the lace-curtained windows, a candle in her hand. When she saw us, she flung open the door.

"What happened?" she cried, her hair askew, her nightdress

too short to touch the ground.

"George got bit by an alligator," I said. Diego and I carried him inside. By now George was very weak, his head falling forward. He did not say a word.

"In here," said Ana Jai, pointing to Captain Clarke's bedroom across from the parlor. Diego and I laid George on the bed.

Ana Jai gasped when she held the candle to his face. George's warm brown skin looked the color of cold oatmeal.

"We're losing him," she cried. "Diego, find a doctor. Mary, get your sister. I need my herbs! Hurry, both of you!"

Thus our sweet dreams of found treasure ended in a living nightmare.

It scared me that Ana Jai called for a doctor since it's something she never does. She has a deep distrust of doctors, on average, and compares their medicinal ways to that of savages. Ana Jai trusts the plants in her herb garden more than doctors themselves.

Nevertheless, Diego did as he was told. He said later he found a doctor by going to the apothecary shop on Centre Street and banging on the door. He didn't know what else to do and banging on that door made him feel like he was doing something. Turns out, a man by the name of Doctor Galt lived upstairs. He sold medicines from the shop below. He heard Diego's banging and eventually opened the door.

Once summoned, Dr. Galt went directly to Captain Clarke's house.

"Everyone I've seen who gets bit by a gator gets a very high fever," Doctor Galt pronounced. "Gators have very dirty mouths with pieces of past dinners, like marsh mice and opossums, trapped between their teeth. Such pestilence may well burn the life out of the boy. He needs a bloodletting."

Ana Jai did not like the idea of extracting what amounted to a bucketful of blood from George's body, the same amount of liquid you'd get from milking a cow.

"A bloodletting will only make him weaker," Ana Jai said.

"But it will release the bad humors," Dr. Galt replied.

Ana Jai frowned, unconvinced.

"I will try my herbs first," she said.

The doctor left, but not before dispensing two more pieces of advice. He said we may have to amputate George's leg. And he advised us to pray.

Ana Jai was all for praying but she also believed in more action. She sent Martha to find echinacea root because she believed that, once boiled, it made a good tea for washing wounds. We used to grow this plant at Mandarin where Ana Jai planted echinacea, with its purple daisylike flowers, around our house. However, no one thought to dig up any echinacea roots before Ana Jai set the house afire.

And she sent me and Abraham Hanahan to find as much holy thistle as possible. Ana Jai says this plant can heal anything. She makes a warm drinking tea from it that tastes completely terrible.

"And don't just bring back the leaves. I need the whole plant to make a strong tea," Ana Jai ordered.

Abraham was often asked to find medicinal herbs when we lived at Mandarin, so for him, this search was nothing new. He grabbed his haversack and we started out.

"Holy thistle grows in sandy soil. We must walk toward the ocean," he said.

My heart sank when I heard this. I was already exhausted from staying up all night, riding to Sadler's Creek, and then returning at dawn with George to Captain Clarke's house. But I dared not complain and plodded along behind Abraham.

"Why you walking so slow?" he asked, frustrated at my pace.

"Just a little tired, is all," I told him.

He shot me a look that said if we had all been in our beds where we belonged last night none of this would have happened.

I started to cry—big, silent tears dripping down my face.

If Abraham saw those tears, they didn't soften his heart or slow his pace, so I spent much of the time walking to the ocean falling behind him, then running to catch up.

By midday we found three holy thistle plants, covered in tiny gray nettles and crowned with purple flowers. They were tucked between two sand dunes. Abraham placed them gently inside his haversack and we headed back.

The sun dipped low in the sky by the time we arrived at Captain Clarke's house. Ana Jai was out back in the kitchen, a large room separated from the rest of the Captain's house by a covered walkway. A pot of echinacea roots bubbled away over a fire in the hearth.

"How's George?" I asked.

"Not good. Martha's with him now. He's feverish,"

She paused and I braced myself for the question I knew was coming.

"Mary, where were you last night?"

Perhaps it was the exhaustion. Certainly it was the worry over what would become of George. Thus, when Ana Jai asked me this question, I burst into tears.

"I'm so sorry," I cried. "We went to search for a treasure Gullah Jack told us about. We didn't tell you because we knew you'd never let us go."

Ana Jai frowned. She stirred the pot of echinacea and

set the spoon on a nearby table. She looked at me crying like a baby.

"Go to bed, Mary," she said. "We'll talk in the morning."

16

Normally, I loved to go to bed the night before my birthday. It was always fascinating to me how you could go to bed, say, age ten and wake up the very next day age eleven. Add to that the fact that waking up on my birthday also meant waking up on Christmas Day, and you can see why, normally, I looked forward to December 25 all year long.

Not this year. This year when I awoke on my birthday I felt doomed, like a bird trapped in a hungry cat's jaws. Today was punishment day for leaving the house in the middle of the night, and I figured I'd be bearing most of Ana Jai's anger since George was sick with fever and Diego was not hers to punish.

I found Ana Jai before the sun came up, sitting downstairs in a rocking chair next to George. He slept fitfully, his breath quick and shallow. Dark circles framed Ana Jai's eyes.

"How is he?" I whispered.

"Not good. Feel how hot he is."

I pressed my hand to George's forehead and felt it burn. Then I took my hand away and it still felt like it was burning.

Ana Jai taught me long ago when your hand burns *after* you take it off someone's forehead, that someone has a bad fever.

"Ana Jai, I'm so sorry." Tears filled my eyes again.

"After a foolish deed there is remorse," she said.

Martha may dislike the African proverbs, but I always found the truth in them strangely comforting. This proverb, however, did not ease my anguish.

"Is George going to die?" I asked.

"I pray not," she sighed. "But look."

Ana Jai pulled back George's quilt. His entire left leg was purple and swollen big as a palm tree trunk.

"We may have to cut off his leg to save his life," she said.

"No," I cried, horrified by the very idea.

As tears flooded my face I wondered again where Father was and why he was never around when his family needed him. He promised to be home by Christmas and here it was Christmas day. There was still no sign him.

Martha came downstairs to sit with George.

"Go get some rest," she said to Ana Jai.

"I will," she said. "Every time he opens his eyes, give him a sip of tea."

"We will," Martha said, as Ana Jai dragged her tired body upstairs to bed.

Martha and I sat quietly with George. Our vigil was interrupted only by the ticking of a clock in Captain Clarke's parlor, its bells sounding the occasional hour.

At one point George stirred like he was having a bad dream.

"Gold," he muttered.

Martha looked at me, dismayed by the utter foolishness of his feverish thoughts.

Diego came in soon after the clock chimed nine times. His feelings were betrayed by the worried look on his face.

"Should I get the doctor again?" he offered.

"No. We need to break the fever and the doctor can't do that any better than we can," Martha said.

Diego joined our quiet vigil. Every so often, Martha pressed a cool, wet cloth to George's sweaty forehead and tried to get him to sip the tea, but mostly we just watched him breathe his short, ragged breaths.

When the clock struck noon, Ana Jai appeared in the doorway.

"Girls, it's time for dinner," she announced, ignoring Diego.

"Ana Jai, I'm not hungry," said Martha.

"Neither am I," I said.

"It's time for dinner," she repeated. And this time the tone in her voice implied we had no choice in the matter.

"I'll stay with George," Diego said.

Martha and I headed into the dining room, where Ana Jai was already seated at the head of the table. We took a seat on either side of her.

There was sliced ham, sweet potatoes, and biscuits for supper, along with Ana Jai's special ambrosia for dessert. It was all laid out on blue china plates belonging to Captain Clarke. Ana Jai's china plates had been packed up tight in cotton baskets and hidden in the woods at Mandarin. Hers came from England, a fact that made us all very proud. I'm sure Captain Clarke's dishes came from there too, because they were equally fine.

But it seemed crazy to be eating dinner and using fancy dishes with George almost dying in the next room. I simply did not have the appetite for it and I wondered how Ana Jai could.

"I'll say the blessing," she said, extending her hands. We all clasped our hands together and bowed our heads.

"Lord, thank you for this meal. Through your grace we were not captured by Patriots and sent into slavery. You have given us shelter to see us through until we get to our next home, Lord. You have also given me three beautiful children and I thank you. They do not appreciate all your blessings, Lord, and even tried to ruin all you've given us through their thoughtless actions. Please forgive them. Through your mercy, George will recover and Zephaniah will make it home safely. For this we pray. Amen."

"Amen," I mumbled.

"That's not fair, Ana Jai," Martha said after the blessing. "I did not sneak out of the house to search for that foolish treasure."

"But you must have known of their plans and did not tell me. That is just as bad as the action itself."

Martha's mouth fell open to a big letter "O," big enough to catch green-headed flies, but no words came out.

And then it dawned on me. There would be no whipping for sneaking out of the house. Instead, as punishment, Ana Jai intended to make us both feel as guilty and selfish as she possibly could. And if George died, that feeling would stay with us a lifetime.

"Here Mary, have some ambrosia. I know it's your favorite dessert. I especially wanted you to have it, you like it so."

Ana Jai said this with a sweetness I know she did not feel, while dishing up a serving of her tangy dessert. I dutifully took a bite, but I could not enjoy it. I could only think of George lying motionless in his sickbed, the fever gripping his body. It was difficult to swallow.

I pushed the orange slices around in my bowl, thinking how this Christmas and birthday turned out so different from how I had imagined it would be. Usually a priest came from St. Augustine on Christmas to say Mass at Mandarin, then we would gather for a special dinner after that. I always received a big birthday present from Father, something he bought just for me on his travels.

But this year, we didn't go to church because no one could think of leaving George. And this year there certainly was no present because there was no Father to bring it. I began to wonder if we'd lose Father just like we may lose George.

As I tried to eat the ambrosia, the front door opened and a man's voice called out, "Hello!"

Little did I know this arrival would add a dramatic turn to the day's events. Although I did know in an instant I wouldn't have to finish my ambrosia.

17

Before we could get up from the table, Captain Clarke stuck his sunburned head into the dining room. He was back from the voyage and he sure looked surprised to see us sitting in his fine dining room eating dinner with his equally fine china.

Ana Jai quickly explained how we left Mandarin, fearing a Patriot attack. (She failed to add that she had also burned our house down.) Captain Clarke welcomed us and pondered the news we brought. In addition to his house in Fernandina, he owned a big indigo plantation in East Florida that he, too, feared Patriots would overrun.

"Where's Zephaniah?" Ana Jai asked.

He explained how Father got off the ship in a small boat back at the entrance to the St. Johns River. He said Father felt he could get home faster that way, instead of coming all the way north to Fernandina then heading back south to Laurel Grove and Mandarin. He said Father was determined to be home by Christmas.

This news set off two emotions in me. I was happy to hear Father was safely back from his voyage, but I was sorely disappointed he didn't walk through that front door with Captain Clarke. Plus, now I had a new worry: would Father run into the Patriots we fled?

George yelled something from his sickbed just then. It sounded a lot like he said, "Gator."

Concern registered in Captain Clarke's eyes as he headed to his bedroom to see my feverish brother lying in his bed. Diego was trying to calm George down.

"Who's this?" the Captain asked.

"My son, George. He was bitten by an alligator," Ana Jai said, following behind Captain Clarke.

"How in the world did that happen?"

Ana Jai did not answer. Instead she looked directly at me, waiting for me to explain to Captain Clarke.

"George must have come too close to a nest of baby alligators," I told him, shifting restlessly from foot to foot. "It happened up by Sadler's Creek."

Thankfully, Captain Clarke did not ask for further details. Ana Jai pulled back the quilt to show George's swollen leg.

"Has a doctor seen him?"

Ana Jai nodded.

"The doctor said the bite is causing the fever. He said we may need to do a bloodletting. Or cut off his leg."

Captain Clarke nodded thoughtfully, taking in the gravity of George's condition. "I've never seen anyone survive an amputation."

Ana Jai nodded in agreement.

"He'll probably walk with a limp the rest of his life . . . if he survives. Stay here as long as you need to, Ana Jai. I'm leaving tomorrow anyway. I need to see if Patriots have laid waste to my indigo plantation."

Captain Clarke excused himself and headed to the kitchen to find something to eat. I wanted to tell him there was some perfectly good ambrosia sitting in a dish on the dining room table, but I didn't want to remind Ana Jai I had not finished mine.

When he left the room, the strength seemed to leave Ana Jai. She sank onto the edge of George's sickbed, looking defeated. I'd never seen Ana Jai look like this before and a wave of fear and guilt rolled through me.

Martha, thankfully, brought us back to the problem at hand.

"Ana Jai, if Father has returned to Laurel Grove, perhaps we should send Abraham Hanahan there to tell him we are here."

Ana Jai looked up as Martha continued.

"Father is going to think the worst has befallen us, since Mandarin is burnt to the ground. He won't have any idea where we've gone. Abraham could leave right now and return tomorrow with Father."

"You're right. Ask Abraham to go. Tell him it is my wish."

Ana Jai returned to nursing George, feeling his forehead and forcing him to take sips of holy thistle tea. She had great faith in her herbs, I knew, but she also feared George might die in spite of them.

18

It took Abraham Hanahan a day and a half to travel to Mandarin and back. He looked exhausted when he walked into the kitchen.

I had just set a pot of holy thistle tea to steeping when a strong nor'easter pushed Abraham through the door. He was cold and wet and stomping his feet to shake water from his clothes.

"Did you find Father?" I asked eagerly.

"No," he said, sounding as tired as he looked. "Where is Ana Jai?"

"With George."

Abraham pulled off his hat and headed out the other kitchen door, the one that lead to the main house.

I followed close behind.

"Ana Jai," he whispered softly when he got to the room where, for a change, George was sleeping quietly instead of thrashing about in a feverish haze. For five days Ana Jai bathed my brother's leg in echinacea tea, hoping to bring down the swelling. In truth, her ministrations seemed to be working because George's leg appeared a little less troubled. Ana Jai looked up, startled, when Abraham called her name.

"I could not find Zephaniah," he said quietly.

Ana Jai nodded.

"But I did find Gullah Jack. He never went to St. Augustine with everyone else. He's been hiding in the woods around Mandarin ever since you gave him his freedom papers. He just walked right up and said hello.

"He told me Patriots arrived shortly after we left. When they saw Mandarin was gone, they crossed the river to Laurel Grove. Made themselves at home there for a day or two."

Ana Jai smiled to herself, justified that Patriots were not far away the night she burned down our house. Then she shook her head, seemingly disgusted at the idea of Patriots living at Laurel Grove.

"Jack says he saw a man he thinks was Zephaniah arrive by boat at Laurel Grove on Christmas Eve, just after the Patriots arrived there," Abraham said. "He says Patriots grabbed the man soon as he got out of his boat. Tied up his hands. Several hours later, Jack says, Patriots forced him back into the boat. They rowed away, heading north."

"They're taking him to Georgia!" I cried.

"Calm down, Mary," Ana Jai ordered. "We're not even sure if this man was Zephaniah."

"They'll kill him!"

"Not likely. Zephaniah is a powerful man. Plus, he's one of their own. If this prisoner is your father, he'll give them what they want."

"What's that?"

"Land, Africans, money. All of which Zephaniah has in abundance. Perhaps they're just trying to scare him."

Somehow, I did not share my mother's confidence in Father's future. And I went looking for the one person who'd be just as worried as me about Father's safety.

19

I found Diego in the barn, brushing King Lear with a fancy brush of Captain Clarke's made from wild boar hair. He stopped grooming when I told him of Father's plight. In fact, he wanted to get in a boat and go to Georgia to look for Father that very instant. I talked him out of this notion, having learned a thing or two about wild ideas and their consequences.

Still, Diego wanted to do something and suggested we return to the docks to be on the lookout for Father. Diego thought we could also talk to people who could tell us of the Patriots and their latest doings and thereby learn news of Father. I thought that a good idea, but I also knew I'd be doing all the talking. Diego was too shy to ask questions of a stranger.

Ana Jai agreed to let me go. But this time, since George couldn't be at the docks to watch us, she insisted Abraham Hanahan spend the day there with me and Diego.

Early the next morning, I pulled my cloak across my shoulders and prepared to leave for the waterfront. Martha stopped me at the front door. She was staying to help with George, but she handed me six ham biscuits wrapped in a cloth. They were still warm.

"You'll get hungry down there waiting," she said, giving me a hug.

Abraham and Diego were waiting for me on the front porch and we walked to the end of Centre Street where the ships come in. Yesterday's nor'easter was over and the day held the promise of warmer weather.

At the waterfront, we sat on bales of Sea Island cotton, damp from yesterday's rain. The cotton would be loaded onto a ship soon and sent to New York City. I sat on my heavy cloak, facing north, looking out at the Cumberland Sound. I could see Georgia in the distance and if I looked behind me, I could see the corner of Captain Clarke's house down Centre Street.

We kept our eyes on everyone who came near us: sailors, shoppers, Africans on errands for their keepers. We also watched for boats approaching on the river. It was slow work.

We ate the salty ham biscuits soon after we got there, more out of boredom than hunger.

"Abraham," Diego said, chewing a biscuit. "You think there's a buccaneers' treasure out there?"

"Maybe."

"Want to go looking for it with me?"

"Diego!" I yelled, crumbs of ham biscuit spitting from my mouth. "How can you even think about that treasure? George may die because of it. It doesn't exist, and if it does, it's trouble. Nothing but trouble."

Diego said nothing more but I knew what he was thinking. He wanted to go searching for that treasure again. Abraham scanned the horizon for boats. He didn't commit to going with Diego one way or the other.

"Look," he said, pointing to a canoe in the distance.

Diego and I studied the small boat as it came closer to shore. Two people were in it, one paddling. The other sat up front. In a few moments we knew neither of these men was Father because they both had brown hair. Father's hair had turned white long ago.

Still, we watched closely as the tiny boat approached the water's edge. The man in front got out, and pulled the canoe high up on shore so it wouldn't float away. Then he reached back into the boat and carefully pulled out a large book and a thin wooden box, tucking them both under his arm. I could tell he didn't want to get them wet. He looked up to see us staring.

"Good day," he called, walking over.

"Good day, sir" I replied. Diego kept his mouth shut tight as an oyster. So did Abraham. I was the only one left to discourse with him.

"Can you tell me where we can get a meal and perhaps a room for the night?"

"Yes, sir. Over there is an ale house." I pointed to an eatery up Centre Street. "They can tell you about a room, too."

"Good," he said, turning to leave.

"What's that you're carrying?" I asked, my imagination getting the better of my manners.

"My work," he said, gently touching the book under his arm. Turns out, he was a naturalist who traveled into the woods to paint birds, flowers, fish, whatever he liked.

"I plan to publish my pictures someday. Would you like to see?"

"Yes," I said, jumping up. The man opened his book and handed me one side to hold while he slowly turned the pages. Diego and Abraham crowded around.

The book was a sketchbook, the likes of which I have yet to see again. My eyes feasted on pages and pages of beautiful drawings, some painted with color, some pencil sketches. There were blue jays and redbirds, ospreys and wild turkeys. There were studies of flowers like yellow lilies from front, back and sideways. And there were pages and pages of all kinds of butterflies.

"Did you draw this?" I asked.

"Everything," he answered proudly.

I enjoyed every picture. They reminded me of an all too familiar world we'd left behind in Mandarin, which made me homesick.

"That's a zebra longwing," I said, pointing to my favorite butterfly.

"You know them?"

I nodded, not willing to explain the zebras at my old home, the home I'd never see again.

The man's traveling companion came up just then, carrying a gun. He did not smile like the young painter.

"Are you going to be here awhile?" he demanded.

I nodded.

"Can you watch our boat?"

At that point Abraham spoke up.

"As long as we're here," he said. Abraham did not want to be responsible for their belongings after that.

The man with the gun scowled at Abraham, but the painter thanked us, still friendly as could be. The two headed off toward the ale house.

"Have you news of the Patriots?" I asked, calling after him.

"No. We've been in the wilderness for weeks," he called back.

I allowed myself a quiet chuckle.

"I can't wait to tell Martha about the handsome painter," I said, knowing full well Martha would have loved to meet him.

Diego looked at me sternly.

"That's not why we're here, Mary."

"I know," I said, a glumness settling over me as I sat back down on the cotton bales to watch the river for any sign of Father.

20

The day we met the painter came and went without Father's return. Same with the next day. By the third day of our wait at the waterfront, panic started to bubble in my stomach like seasickness. Where could Father be? If the Patriots had him, would they hurt him? I worried I'd never see Father again and I swallowed hard trying to keep down my fears.

On the third day the sky was clear blue and the wind at the waterfront blew its warm breath softly against my cheek. The bales of Sea Island cotton had shipped out so we settled ourselves on some sacks marked "Sugar." Diego blew a screechy tune from a penny whistle he'd bought at the dry goods store.

"Abraham, do you think Patriots have killed Father?" I asked him this question every day and he always gave me the same answer.

"No," he said.

It reassured me that Abraham had not given up hope, even though he had no way of knowing any better than the rest of us if Father would return safely.

As the day grew warmer I took off my cloak. I folded it into a pillow, sat on top of it, and leaned against the sugar sacks. Then I closed my eyes and took a short nap in the warm December sun.

I dreamed I was back at Mandarin playing "King of the Castle" with Diego. We played this game on a particularly big oyster mound that was so old it had weeds growing out of it like a hill.

"I'm Queen of the Castle and you're the dirty rascal," I'd shout to Diego from the top of the mound. He'd scramble up and try to push me off. We'd wrestle like this for hours.

As the shells decayed, they turned into a fine white powder that covered our skin and clothes. We usually took a dunk in the river, clothes and all, to clean off before heading home.

"Mary, wake up," said Diego, jostling my shoulder. "Look."

I opened my eyes, squinting in the sunlight, and saw two men in a boat, rowing toward us. I could only see their backs as they sat side by side, each with an oar in their hands, rowing. But this time the boat came from a different direction than the canoe carrying the handsome painter. This time, it came from Georgia.

Abraham was already standing by the water's edge when Diego and I joined him.

"It's Zephaniah," he said, simply.

Tears welled up in my eyes as I waited for the boat to row closer to shore.

Slowly, they came, until finally I could see the side of Father's face. Not too far from shore, he turned around, saw us waiting, and waved.

We all waved back. When the boat was a few yards offshore, Abraham waded into the water and pulled it in. Father, his black suit very wrinkled, stowed his oar and turned around.

"Ahoy, mates," he yelled.

"Ahoy, Father," we yelled back.

He hopped out of the boat, the water up to his knees, and sloshed toward us laughing, his arms outstretched. Diego and I ran to meet him. I jumped into Father's arms and kissed his neck, knocking his straw sun hat into the water. He tasted salty, smelled sweaty. Diego retrieved the hat, then hugged Father's waist.

"Where have you been?" I asked.

"I was detained," he answered.

Just then the other man in the boat yelled to Father. The man looked familiar, but I couldn't recall where I'd seen him.

"Remember our agreement," the man called.

"I remember," said Father.

"Who is that" I asked.

"John Houston McIntosh," Father replied. And then it dawned on me. I had seen that face before. That man was the merchant who told Ana Jai Patriots burned down the Fatios' plantation.

"He came to Mandarin selling his wares," I told Father. "Was he selling you something?"

"In a way he was, Mary," Father said, putting me down. I grabbed his hand, unwilling to ever let him go again.

"Where are George and Martha? And Ana Jai?" he asked.

Diego and I exchanged a quick look.

"We're all staying at Captain Clarke's house," I said. "We have a lot to tell you."

"And I have a lot to tell you," he replied.

21

In the short time it took to walk to Captain Clarke's house, I told Father how Ana Jai freed all her Africans and how we fled Mandarin, fearing a Patriot attack.

"Ana Jai burned down the house," I blurted out. "Including the Africans' cabins."

Father stopped short, surprised at the news. Then, of all things, he laughed.

"She did?" he said looking at Abraham Hanahan. Abraham nodded, smiling back.

"It's not funny," I said, trying to figure out why Father was laughing.

"Your mother has always been her own woman," he said. "It's her house. If she wanted to burn it down, she could."

"But where will we live?"

"We'll work something out," he said and started walking again.

Then Diego told Father how he saved King Lear from the Patriots by putting him on Ana Jai's riverboat. Father was thrilled.

"Diego, you have a gift with horses. I am so proud of you."

Neither of us, though, could bring ourselves to tell Father about George. We didn't plan not to tell him, exactly, but we just didn't bring it up right then. I think we were both afraid of explaining how we sneaked out of the house in the middle of the night. Father would find out soon enough.

The front door flew open as we walked up the steps to Captain Clarke's house. Martha ran out and threw her arms around Father's neck, smothering him with kisses.

"Where have you been?" she demanded.

"Dealing with Patriots," he said.

Father looked up to see Ana Jai standing in the doorway.

"Hello, Zephaniah," she said quietly.

"Hello, Ana Jai." He stepped forward and hugged her. And remarkably, Ana Jai allowed him to do it. My heart soared.

"Where's George?" he asked, realizing his entire family—except George—was standing on Captain Clarke's front porch.

I dreaded this moment, and I'm sure Martha and Diego did too.

"In here," Ana Jai replied, stepping back into Captain Clarke's house. She showed Father into the dark bedroom where George lay in a deep sleep.

Father knelt by his side. "What happened?" he whispered.

"He was bitten by an alligator. Almost lost his leg," Ana Jai said. "The bite caused a powerful fever that nearly killed him. He's only now cooling off."

I was grateful Ana Jai did not tell Father just then

exactly how George came to be bitten by a gator. That would come later. Right now, she was like us, happy to take in the sight of him. And he felt the same about us, grateful we were alive and together again.

George woke up that evening. The first person he saw was Father, who had not left his bedside since walking into Captain Clarke's house. We were all there actually, because Ana Jai wasn't leaving George either, and me and Martha and Diego weren't leaving Father. So we all crowded into Captain Clarke's bedroom. Ana Jai and Father sat in chairs on either side of George. Diego and Martha and me sat on the floor. From time to time Ana Jai would ask someone to go to the kitchen for biscuits or water or something, but mostly we just sat in that room. There was a lot to talk about.

John Houston McIntosh, it turned out, was the leader of the Patriots. And, indeed, the day he stopped by Mandarin pretending to be a traveling merchant he was really checking out Ana Jai's plantation to see who lived there. He told Father the money he made selling wares as a traveling merchant helped buy gunpowder for the Patriots.

Then Father told us how McIntosh and some other Patriots took him to Georgia. He says the whole time he was there, they argued.

Patriots argued that Spain had to give up its Florida territory. They said Spain was just too far away and didn't have enough soldiers to protect it anymore. Father, realizing the truth of this argument, agreed La Florida was heading for a change. The way he figured it, we were better off joining the Patriots than trying to fight them.

But Father argued with them about allowing freed Africans to remain free in Florida. "McIntosh believes all freed Negroes and mulattoes should be made slaves again,"

Father said. "In the end, I agreed to call myself a Patriot so they'd let me go. But we disagree on the future of freed Africans."

Ana Jai shook her head. I don't think she trusted anyone, not even Father, when it came to her freedom or the freedom of her children.

"I've decided to try and change the way these Patriots think," Father explained. He hoped to convince them that freed Africans and mulattoes should remain free once Florida became a state.

In the meantime, Father announced he bought a new plantation from, of all people, John Houston McIntosh. He said it was on Fort George Island. This meant it was located closer to Fernandina and the Atlantic Ocean, not as remote as Laurel Grove and Mandarin. Father said this was important if we ever needed to sail away in a hurry again.

"We'll call it Kingsley Plantation," he said, pointedly "because *all* the Kingsley's will live there."

He looked directly at Ana Jai. She did not protest. My mother may insist on doing things herself, but even she knew she was no match for the Patriots. For them, she needed Father's protection. And even with it, I don't think Ana Jai was fully convinced Patriots would allow her to remain free.

"What will we grow on the new plantation?" I asked.

"Rice," Father said. "And some Sea Island cotton and sugar cane. I'll still run my trading ships. But from now on, George, you're coming with me. I need you to take on more responsibility in my business affairs."

George smiled broadly. I swear he would have jumped out of bed and danced a jig if he had been strong enough. Martha smiled, too. She was pleased Kingsley Plantation wasn't as deep in the wilderness as Mandarin and Laurel

Grove. She hoped to meet some "gentry" there.

Even Diego was smiling, and I knew exactly why. He liked the idea of living closer to Amelia Island. Diego was going to search for that treasure again.

Of course, I was smiling too, especially on the inside. My whole body felt warm and cozy because my family was really a family again.

Author's Historical Note

The *Treasure of Amelia Island* is historical fiction. This means the setting and many of the characters are real, including Ana Jai, Zephaniah, George, Martha, and Mary Kingsley.

I always wondered what life was like for the children of such a powerful mother, so I imagined the dialogue and many of the scenes in this book. I also created the character of Diego, and changed the ages of the Kingsley children, making them older than they really were in 1813. Still, whenever I fictionalized the family's history, I tried to keep true to their time period.

Here's what we know: Zephaniah freed Ana Jai and their children in 1811. A short time later, Ana Jai took the children and moved across the river from Laurel Grove to her own plantation. The name of that plantation has been lost to time, so I named it Mandarin.

Ana Jai and her children did not live at Mandarin long before Patriot raids threatened their security. When she fled Mandarin, historians say, she burned it to the ground. From

Mandarin, Ana Jai and the children returned to Zephaniah. They all moved to Kingsley Plantation on Fort George Island, which still exists in northeast Florida today as a park run by the National Park Service.

The Kingsleys remained at Kingsley Plantation for twenty-three years. During much of that time, Zephaniah wrote articles and tried to convince lawmakers to allow freed people of color to remain free when Florida became a state. But by 1837 Kingsley realized state lawmakers were not going to agree to this. He was afraid that when he died, his family would be forced into slavery again. That year he moved Ana Jai, George, their fourth child, John Maxwell, and many of their freed slaves to Haiti, a country ruled by former slaves. He thought they'd be much safer there.

Martha and Mary did not go to Haiti. They were both married to wealthy, white men—gentry—and they stayed with their husbands in Jacksonville. Florida entered the United States of America as a slave state on March 3, 1845.

Finally, legend has it, the pirate treasure is still buried somewhere on Amelia Island near the town of Fernandina Beach. A chain hanging from a tall oak tree is said to mark the treasure's location—that is, if you can find the right tree.

Reader's Guide

The Treasure of Amelia Island

by M.C. Finotti

Chapter Pre-reading Questions and Predictions

As you read *The Treasure of Amelia Island,* here are some questions for each chapter to help you think about the story. Don't worry about whether your answers are right or wrong. What's important is that you are thinking about the book and staying engaged in it!

Prologue: What do you think will be the central conflict of this book?

Chapter 1: Why do the children call Ana Jai by her name and not "mother"?

Chapter 2: Will the Kingsley family be reunited and live together again?

Chapter 3: Will the drowning man Mary and Diego pull out of the water survive?

Chapter 4: Will Gullah Jack turn out to be a good guy or a bad guy?

Chapter 5: Do you think the story Jack conjured up about Coosawhatchie is true?

Chapter 6: Will the Patriots harm the Kingsleys?

Chapter 7: Do you believe Gullah Jack's story about the treasure?

Chapter 8: Do you think the traveling merchant was a spy for the Patriots?

Chapter 9: Do you think Ana Jai is overreacting by rushing off to St. Augustine?

Chapter 10: Will Ana Jai be able to keep the Patriots out of Mandarin?

Chapter 11: Do you agree with Ana Jai's decision to burn her plantation to the ground?

Chapter 12: Will Mary and Diego search for the treasure? Will they find it?

Chapter 13: Do you think Martha was wrong for not telling her mother what George, Mary, and Diego were about to do?

Chapter 14: What will Ana Jai do when the children return home?

Chapter 15: Will George survive the gator attack?

Chapter 16: Should Ana Jai have punished Mary more for sneaking out of the house?

Chapter 17: Will Abraham Hanahan find Zephaniah?

Chapter 18: Will the Patriots kill Zephaniah?

Chapter 19: Will Diego go hunting for the treasure again?

Chapter 20: How will Zephaniah react when he learns Ana Jai set her house on fire?

Chapter 21: Will Zephaniah be able to change the way the Patriots think about slavery?

Discussion Questions

1. Historical fiction is like marshmallows in a cup of hot chocolate. It sweetens history and helps it come alive for readers. Good historical fiction is also true to the historical facts. For example, *The Treasure of Amelia Island* does not ignore the fact that Ana Jai, a freed woman of color, kept enslaved people. Why do you think she did this?

2. Why do you think the Patriot Rebellion was an important milestone in Florida history? Do you think Spain should have tried harder to keep to La Florida? What would Florida be like today if it were still a Spanish territory?

3. Who do you think are the three most important characters in this book? How did they change during the course of the story?

4. What was your favorite chapter in this book? What was its central idea? Explain why you liked it.

5. What three questions would you like to ask the author of this book?

Essays and Projects

1. Write an expository essay about how present-day Florida is different from Florida in 1813. Choose from one of these areas: transportation, government, education, or medicine.

2. Write a narrative account about playing in the Redbird Nest in 1813 with a friend. What would you have done up there? Use your creative thinking to make your story different from the scenes in the book.

3. Create a chart that compares and contrasts slavery on a plantation in Florida in 1813 to slavery during that same period on a plantation in Virginia. Could slaves in Virginia earn their freedom? What was the cash crop in Virginia? What was the cash crop in Florida?

4. The Kingsley children learned to read using Aesop's Fables. Do some research on who Aesop was and read three of his fables. Write an essay about Aesop that explains why he pretended many of his stories were about animals, not people.

5. Pretend Hollywood wants to make a movie about *The Treasure of Amelia Island* and a producer needs your help planning it. Find five items in the book the producer will need in the movie. Research exactly what those items looked like in 1813. Draw them on a poster and present your poster to your class.

6. Pretend you are Ana Jai Kingsley and you just found out your children sneaked out of the house in the middle of the night. Write a narrative account telling your chil-

dren how disappointed you are in their actions. Tell them how you plan to discipline them for this dangerous behavior.

7. Research the type of money used in Spanish Florida in the 1700s and 1800s. Create a pamphlet about the money that includes your drawings of the different types of coins.

8. Research the history of ambrosia. Create a tri-fold with three different ambrosia recipes. Be sure and list the ingredients. Draw pictures. Try to make one version of the recipe at home or for your class.

9. Read the author's historical note at the end of the book. Pretend you are Ana Jai or George Kingsley and you now live in Haiti. Write a letter to Martha or Mary back in Jacksonville, Florida. Tell them about your new life in Haiti.

10. Read the author's historical note at the end of the book. Pretend you are Martha or Mary Kingsley. Write a letter to Ana Jai or George in Haiti telling them how your life has changed now that Florida is part of the United States of America.

11. Create a detailed treasure map showing how to find the pirate treasure that's said to be buried on Amelia Island. Make the paper look old by dying it in a cup of strong tea and letting it dry. Draw the map on the dried paper.

12. Research medicinal plants and herbs. Create a poster showing what five of these plants look like. Explain how they were used to cure patients in the 1800s.

13. Pretend you are John Houston McIntosh, the leader of the Patriots. Write a persuasive essay explaining why Florida should no longer be a Spanish territory and should instead become part of the United States of America.

14. Research Christmas customs in Colonial times. What foods did people eat during the holidays? How did they decorate their homes? Did they give gifts? Create a poster to show what you learned.

15. Create a T-chart. On one side write twenty historical facts about Florida in 1813 found in this book. On the other side, write twenty points of historical fiction.

Here are some other books from Pineapple Press on related topics. For a complete catalog, write to Pineapple Press, P.O. Box 3889, Sarasota, Florida 34230-3889, or call (800) 746-3275. Or visit our website at www.pineapplepress.com.

Kidnapped in Key West by Edwina Raffa and Annelle Rigsby. Twelve-year-old Eddie Malone is living a carefree life, swimming and fishing in the Florida Keys in 1912, when his world is suddenly turned upside down. His father, a worker on Henry Flagler's Over-Sea Railroad, is thrown into jail for stealing the railroad payroll. Eddie sets out for Key West with his faithful dog, Rex, on a daring mission to prove his father's innocence. Eddie finds the real thieves, but they kidnap him and lock him aboard their sailboat. As the boat moves swiftly away from Key West, Eddie realizes he's in serious trouble. Can he escape their clutches in time to foil their next plot and prove his pa's innocence? A Teacher's Activity Guide is also available, with activities to help students learn more about Key West and Flagler's Over-Sea Railroad. Includes references to the Sunshine State Standards.

Escape to the Everglades by Edwina Raffa and Annelle Rigsby. Based on historical fact, this young adult novel tells the story of Will Cypress, a half-Seminole boy living among his mother's people during the Second Seminole War. He meets Chief Osceola and travels with him to St. Augustine. A Teacher's Activity Guide is also available, filled with activities to help students learn more about Florida and the Seminoles. Includes references to the Sunshine State Standards.

Blood Moon Rider by Zack C. Waters. When his Marine father is killed in WWII, young Harley Wallace is exiled to the Florida cattle ranch of his grandfather. The murder of a cowman and the disappearance of Grandfather Wallace lead Harley and his new friend, Beth, on a wild ride through the swamps into the midst of a conspiracy of evil that involves a top-secret war mission in the Gulf of Mexico.

Solomon by Marilyn Bishop Shaw. Eleven-year-old Solomon Freeman and his parents, Moses and Lela, survive the Civil War, gain their freedom, and gamble their dreams, risking their very existence on a homestead in the remote environs of north central Florida. Young Solomon learns to ride a marshtackie horse and helps round up a herd of wild cattle.

A Land Remembered: Student Edition by Patrick D. Smith. This well-loved, best-selling novel tells the story of three generations of MacIveys, a Florida family battling the hardships of the frontier. They rise from dirt-poor cracker life to the wealth and standing of real estate tycoons. Now available to young readers in two volumes. Teachers' manuals for both elementary and middle schools are available.

Hunted Like a Wolf: The Story of the Seminole War by Milton Meltzer. Award-winning young adult book that offers a look at the events, players, and political motives leading to the Second Seminole War. It explores the Seminoles' choices and sacrifices and the treachery of the U.S. during that harsh time.